Sophie

About Reconciliation

Debby Bradley

Liguori
LIGUORI, MISSOURI

Illustrated by
Lula Guzmán

Dedication

Grateful
for love and support from my husband, Bill,
and my children, Claire Marie,
Teman John Kaiser, and Molly Renee.

Blessed
to have as my first religious examples
Fr. Bill Vos and Ade Ledermann.

Thankful
to have witnessed the inspiration of these who have
joined the communion of saints: Kenneth Besetzny,
Judith Batton, Helen Marais, and John Kaiser.

Imprimi Potest:
Harry Grile, CSsR, Provincial
Denver Province, The Redemptorists

Published by Liguori Publications
Liguori, Missouri 63057

To order, call 800-325-9521
www.liguori.org

p ISBN: 978-0-7648-2345-9
e ISBN: 978-0-7648-6866-5

Liguori Publications, a nonprofit corporation, is an apostolate of The Redemptorists. To learn more about The Redemptorists, visit Redemptorists.com.

Printed in the United States of America
17 16 15 14 13 / 5 4 3 2 1
First Edition

There once was a little girl.
Her name was Sophie.
Sophie wondered about many things.

Sophie had a fight with her friend Sarah.

Sophie felt bad.
She wondered how she could
make things better.

Sophie told Mommy,
"I was mean to Sarah. I don't want her to
be mad at me anymore. What can I do?"

Mommy said, "You can tell Sarah how you feel. She'd like to know you're sorry and that you feel bad about what you did.

"Sarah will be happy to know you care about her and that you'll try to be a nicer friend next time."

13

Mommy continued,
"You know, Sophie, in your religion
class you've been preparing for the
sacrament of reconciliation."

Sophie
nodded.

15

"Reconciliation is a great place to talk about things like this. You can tell Fr. John about your problem with Sarah and how you feel about it.

"God will forgive anything you do
if you're really sorry and promise
to try not to do it again.

"Fr. John will talk to you about ways to keep your promise, and then he'll help you pray about it so you can make a fresh start."

Sophie thought that
was a good idea.

23

Reconciliation is such a big
word that Sophie had thought
it must be just for grown-ups.
But all it really means
is making things right.

Sophie liked Fr. John and
was excited about reconciliation.

Sophie felt better.

She was ready to tell Sarah
she was sorry for being mean to her.

She was ready to
make a fresh start!

Sophie Wonders
About the Sacraments

Sophie Wonders About Anointing
Paperback 823411 • eBook 868672

Sophie Wonders About Baptism
Paperback 823473 • eBook 868856

Sophie Wonders About Confirmation
Paperback 823497 • eBook 868849

Sophie Wonders About Eucharist
Paperback 823398 • eBook 868689

Sophie Wonders About Holy Orders
Paperback 823435 • eBook 868658

Sophie Wonders About Marriage
Paperback 823510 • eBook 868863

Sophie Wonders About Reconciliation
Paperback 823459 • eBook 868665

To order, visit Liguori.org
or call 800-325-9521